# At the Water's Edge

Stories by
Ann Partridge, Sarah Bella, Lisamarie
Lamb, Carol R. Ward, Amanda Buxton,
Jo-Anne Russell, Jamie DeBree, Heidi
Sutherlin and Jaimie Krycho

At the Water's Edge
ISBN 9781937477837

Compiled by Jamie DeBree & Heidi Sutherlin
Edited by Carol R. Ward
Cover art by Heidi Sutherlin

# Table of Contents

# Water's Edge
## by Ann Partridge

Em considered just walking into the water until it closed in over her head. Not that it would really work like that, she knew. At some point she would have to force herself to sink to the bottom and keep from rising to the surface and swimming back to shore.

She felt heavy enough to sink like a stone. Heavy with grief. The loss of Robbie seemed to weight her limbs, her heart and her head. She felt unable to move or feel anything. This trek to the shore was the first unnecessary thing she had done since he was killed.

She watched the swell and roll as the waves formed again and again. The repetitive motion was like watching time go by, or life itself. The absence of Robbie in the world hadn't made the waves cease and neither would her death. The sun's last rays marked a bright path on the water leading towards Sorrow Island as it began its descent behind the shadowed cliffs there. It was almost an invitation to follow the light.

The colour was fading from the sky, making it harder to pick out the horizon. Only Sorrow Island separated lake from sky. Sorrow Island, how fitting should she end her days on the way there.

The breeze no longer cooled her cheeks and the waves had slowed to a gently rocking lullaby. Em took one step towards the water when a note echoing across the lake touched her memory. Stopping to listen, she could make out the haunting melancholy of bagpipes over the soft swishing of the waves.

The sound took her back to the day she had met Robbie. Em and her sister Anna had been shopping when they heard some commotion out on the street. Stepping out of the shop they saw a parade of Pipe Bands and Highland Dancers making their way down the main street towards the park. Out of curiosity, Em and her sister had followed the parade and discovered the Highland Games. It was an entertaining event on a sparkling summer day and became one to remember after she met Robbie in the tented eating area.

God that man looked great in a kilt. He had been so full of life. Who had known that pipers could be incredibly sexy? He coined her nickname that very first day. He decided Em, instead of being short for Emma, was short for Emerald because of her eyes. He captured her heart just like that and had never done anything to alter her feelings. Except go to Afghanistan.

She didn't know if it was the haunting sound of the pipes or the memories of her time together with Robbie that made her throat tighten and released her long dammed-up tears. The two of them had traded passionate love letters that they would have been too embarrassed to share with anyone else. Em had been amazed at how much easier it was to pour her real feelings out on paper than to vocalize them face-to-face with Robbie. Sure they e-mailed back and forth and even had hilarious conversations face-to-face on Skype, but she had treasured their written communication for its depth of feeling.

As her silent tears made shining tracks down her cheeks and fell to join the waves lapping at her feet, Em let herself feel rage at the futility of Robbie's death. He had been killed by "friendly fire," by people from his own side of the conflict. He only had three more weeks to complete his tour of duty and then he would have been coming home to marry his emerald-eyed girl.

It seemed impossible to her that Robbie's voice would never again be heard in the world. Almost two weeks after his death, Em received the final love letter from her beloved piper. It made her question if his death, funeral and the surrounding formalities were real. It sent her over the edge into a black abyss, almost madness. Today was her first foray back into the light of the world and she didn't know if she could live with Robbie's large absence, or if she wanted to. Sorrow Island seemed to be calling her name.

Em inhaled on a sob, bowed her head down under the weight of the hurt and closed her tear-filled eyes. She let the sound of the waves and the pipes wash over her. The mist from the waves gently touched her tear-soaked face. She felt the heaviness of the pain pulling her to her knees. Finally, kneeling on the damp sand, head bowed almost to the ground, she keened aloud and rocked with anguish.

When she next opened her eyes, it was dark. When her eyes adjusted to the absence of light, she realized that she could still make out the silvery tips of the waves breaking against the shore. Shakily she got to her feet and thought there would be nothing easier than slipping out into that darkness. As she stepped towards her fate, the tones of the pipes reached her once again. They tugged at her broken heart. Something else tugged at her, too. She felt the stirring of life inside her.

The baby chose this moment to make Em aware of its presence. A child. Hers and Robbies'. Some part of Robbie to belong to her future, to give her a future, to feel uplifted by the sound of the pipes again, to have someone to share it with.

Em took one last look at the silvery waves. Turning away from the water, she took a step towards home.

###

## About the Author

Ann Partridge is a member of Northumberland Scribes, a writers' group which helps motivate her to sit at her computer and put thoughts into words. She is a compulsive reader and enjoys making wine.

# London
## by Sarah Bella

The frothy ocean mocks me from my place in the rocky sand and I sigh before sinking to my knees. Wetness soaks through my jeans as the sand rises up to greet me. I watch as the waves lap at the shore, coming home.

New Hampshire is bleak this time of year, that awkward phase between fall and winter. The leaves have all fallen but the clouds hungrily hold onto their snow. The roadsides are dirty, remnants of summer and beach sand clinging to the shoulders. All the flowers have faded, spoiled seed heads waiting expectantly for spring.

The wind bites into the bared skin of my face and hands and I clutch my jacket more tightly against my chest. It whips my hair violently away from my face, stinging my cheeks. My eyes burn as I hold back my tears.

London is so far, and yet, I feel as though I should be able to see it, just on the other side of the ocean.

Months apart, months of text messages and emails, of video chats and touching ourselves because we couldn't reach one another. All that these months apart have led to is heartbreak.

A bomb scare. A train station.

And then suddenly, the scare was serious. Deadly serious.

And I hate this ocean; this ocean that's kept me apart from him. I hate this sand and I pound my fists into it. The wind howls passed my ears and tears stain my cheeks as I unleash my fury onto the undeserving beach.

I realize with a start that the keening sound I hear isn't the wind, but me. My cries are screams, so pained that it hurts me more to hear them. But I can't stop and I scream and beat the sand with my fists until my throat is raw and my shoulders sore.

All this pain and sadness, it won't bring him back. It can't cross the ocean. So I fling it out to the waves for them to carry away from me. I climb back to my feet and kick at the pebbles littering the shore. I kick them and watch with no sense of satisfaction as they plunk into the water.

My fists are clenched so tightly they ache and my knuckles cry for relief, but the pain grounds me. It reminds me that I'm still alive even if he isn't.

# Her House
## by Lisamarie Lamb

It had been there; she had seen it.

It couldn't have simply vanished, it couldn't have simply disappeared.

It had *been* there.

A house. A large, white house at the top of the cliff jutting out over the water, perfect with the sun setting behind it in the late afternoon haze, the chimneys puffing smoke, the atmosphere surrounding it warm and enticing and inviting.

And now it was gone.

She had only blinked, and she had lost it.

She dug her hands into her pockets, the thin material doing nothing to protect her from the cooling air. She saw her own breath as she exhaled, one long sigh of disappointment, of confusion, of longing.

It was *her* house. She had dreamed it so many times, or remembered it so many times, both were the same to her, and now it existed, she had seen it. It *had* been there. And the grief at having lost such a precious thing rivaled the grief she had felt when… what? She couldn't remember, but there was something, wasn't there? Something catching at her memory, calling for her attention, but never quite loud enough, never quite there.

It saddened her. Both the memory, whatever it was, and the loss. She felt it deep, dark and dangerous, eating at her, gnawing away at the core of her. It maddened her that she couldn't grasp it, couldn't attach any substance to it.

She kicked at the foam brought to her feet by the sea itself. It split into a million foamy bubbles and spread itself over her shoe, bursting and disappearing, only this time she could see it happening. With the house, that beautiful house, it was different; she had missed its leaving. One moment it had been there and then, with an involuntary blink, it was gone. She could see it now, the inside of it, wood paneled and warm, open fires in every room, oversized furniture, antique and kitsch. Comfortable. The overwhelming feeling was of comfort and of happiness.

The garden was long and green and full of trees, big trees, old trees, trees that had been there before the house, before the road, before her. Trees that could be climbed and that had houses built into the strong branches, branches that bowed just a little more each year until some of them reached the lush grass beneath. They were just touching, just tickling, the leaves and blades of green melding together to become one natural canopy.

The kitchen smelled of baking, cakes and biscuits and roast dinners. A grandmother was cooking, enjoying it, wanting to please. She wiped her floury hands on a floury apron, the dust rose up and floated, suspended for a moment before drifting back down. It coated the same hands that had brushed it away and coated the sturdy wooden table that was carved with initials and names and dates. Carved with *her* initials if she could only remember what they were. Carved with *her* dates.

The hallway was big, wide and open, bright with a broad open staircase that curved up and around and away, beckoning weary travelers as they stood wondering at the perfectness of it all. The expansive stairs, a playground for children who could lie across the steps and stare up at the plaster shapes and shadows on the ceiling, so far up it felt like the sky, summoned them up; *rest with us, rest and revive.*

She knew they did.

She knew because she remembered.

It *was* her house, after all.

And as she stood and stared and waited for it to reappear, the hours grew long and the day short and the night came. Still she stood, the waves coming closer and closer, engulfing her feet, her ankles, almost her knees, and then falling away, changing their mind and retreating, only to gather themselves to try another assault.

But she didn't notice. Time went on and on and always on and she stood on the beach or in the sea when the tide was in the mood to climb further up the sand and splash against her legs. The seasons came and went and the years came and went and she stood still.

Sometimes she saw the house and it pleased her. But any thought of going to it was frozen in place with the joy of finding it again. Happiness paralyzed her and she could only smile and half remember and let a tear slide down her cheek and drip, drop into the sea at her feet.

Sometimes the house was gone and that was when the melancholy came. And then she *couldn't* move since she might miss its reappearance.

And sometimes she saw people in the house and she never knew whether she was happy or sad about it. It is only when the people are there that she remembers that she died a long time ago. She is no longer wanted or needed in that house, the house she loved and loves still and cannot leave despite everything, despite *knowing*.

And sometimes, only sometimes, someone from the house would see her. A little girl lived in that house long years after she did, and *she* saw her. Maybe twice a year, maybe once every two years, maybe not for a decade or more, but she saw. She told her parents and then she told her brother. She told her husband and then she told her children. She told her grandchildren and she planned to tell her great grandchildren although she never met them.

It was a good story. It lived on long after she did. After they all did.

And still she stands and waits.

###

## About the Author

Lisamarie was five when she wrote her first short story - it involved a car going over a cliff, Jessica Fletcher and the Phantom Raspberry Blower. It didn't have much of a plot (he did it, she solved it) but it did have rather colourful (crayon) illustrations and it made her realize that writing was what she wanted to do.

At 12 she wrote her first novel during the school summer holidays. Loosely based on the Famous Five, with a bit of James Bond thrown in, it was an adventure story and her English teacher made her read some of it in class. And that's when she realised that she wanted people to hear her stories and read her work.

Throughout the intervening years, Lisamarie has written various short stories, plays, poems and novels in different genres, including romance and children's books. She has a blog that showcases flash fiction at www.themoonlitdoor.blogspot.com.

# Siren's Call
## by Carol R. Ward

*Save me . . .*

She called it the shore, rather than the beach.
Beaches conjured up visions of sand and sun and
gently lapping, warm tropical waves - fruity drinks
with happy little umbrellas in them brought to you by
sloe eyed cabana boys who promised so much more
than just a cool drink.

No, this was a shore. There was precious little
sand, only grit and rock. The water was cold and grey
and crashed angrily along the coast. There were no
drinks to be had, unless you thought to bring a ther-
mos of tea or coffee with you and she seldom remembered to do that.

*Save me . . .*

It was here she first saw him. Here that she found
him - half in, half out of the water, naked, so cold to
the touch she was afraid he was already dead. But

then he opened his eyes and it was too late. She was caught. Mesmerized. His.

She helped him to her cabin, laying him down on her bed. Although she knew he'd been injured, she could find no sign of it. When she turned to get a blanket to cover him, his hand shot out, grasping hers, pulling her down on top of him.

*I need you . . .*

They made love with an intensity she had never experienced before. He filled all the empty places inside her, binding her to him. Their soft cries filled the night – hers of completion; his of possession.

He was otherworldly in his beauty and she marveled that out of all the miles of coastline he'd chosen her small stretch. He'd chosen her. She never realized how lonely she'd been, living her life in isolation on the shore, until *he* came to share it with her.

*I need you . . .*

She made a modest living writing nature articles for a wildlife magazine, but after his arrival she suddenly found herself yearning to finish the novel she started a long time ago. A lifetime ago. He was her inspiration.

It was as though they'd always been together. They were inseparable, save for twice a day when the tides turned. He would stand, immersed in the cold water of the bay, arms raised to the heavens, while she watched from the shore. She could no longer imagine her life before him. She did not want to imagine her life after he disappeared again.

*Wait for me . . .*

They never talked about it, but she'd known from the beginning he could not remain. He stayed for a month, from one full moon to the next, helping her with her small chores during the day, making sweet love to her during the night.

While she thought of him as hers, as she was his, there was a part of him that she could not lay claim to. It was the same part that lay with the water, the tides, the ocean. It pulsed in his blood, was one with the spirit she had grown to love.

*Wait for me . . .*

He was not of the earthly realm, his place lay elsewhere. In her heart she knew he hadn't wanted to leave, but the pull of the sea was too great to resist. He promised it was not the end, that they'd be together, and she believed him.

She watched from the shore as he left, striding naked into the cold water, oblivious to the pull of the waves. Perhaps he felt a different pull. He turned once, a shared glance that said everything mere words could not, then he was gone. The wind dried her tears as she stood there, watching until it was too dark to see. Only then did she make her way back to her cabin. Alone.

*Come to me . . .*

She began spending more and more time at the shore, ignoring the wind when it whipped her hair away from her face, the salt laden air as it dampened her clothing, the cold as it seeped into her bones. If she held perfectly still and listened carefully, she could still hear his voice in the wind coming off the water.

Sometimes, when the water was calmer and the wind was still, she would pace along the shore. Her eyes would seek for signs of his return; of course she never found any. Now and then she would stop and stare into the water, trying to discern shapes beneath its surface.

*Come to me . . .*

At night she would curl up in her cold and lonely bed, sleeping only fitfully. The nights she dreamed of him were almost worse than the nights she didn't, for when she woke in the morning it was without him and the ache would be worse than ever.

He had promised they'd be together and she clung to that promise.

*Come to me . . .*

The thought was insidious, winding through her mind like the kudzu vines amongst the rocks – perhaps he was testing her. Perhaps she was supposed to go to him. Perhaps he was the one waiting for her.

She stood on the shore looking out over the grey, angry water, waves crashing on the rocks. He was out there, she could feel it. Shoulders back and head held high, she stepped forward.

*Destiny . . .*

*Finally . . .*

###

## About the Author

Residing in Cobourg, Ontario, Carol has always had a love of writing. She grew up reading old copies of Edgar Rice Burroughs and Robert E. Howard so it's no wonder her first love is fantasy and science fiction.

She always believed she was meant to be a writer of short stories, however her stories tended to be rather long. They also tended to have a romantic thread running through them. Finally caving in to the inevitable, she embraced her genre of began writing novels of fantasy/science fiction adventure with a dash of romance thrown into the mix. She has never regretted it.

Today she writes a variety of prose: non-fiction, flash fiction, short stories, and novels – in a variety of genres: humour, horror, contemporary, romance, science fiction, and fantasy. Having recently discovered a love of poetry forms, she explores a new form of poetry every week.

Visit Carol on her blog, Random Thoughts of the Writerly Kind.
http://randomwriterlythoughts.blogspot.com.

# The Loch
## by Amanda Buxton

There was a rustling behind her, but Mona didn't bother turning around from the water's edge. She was used to people watching her while she worked.

Watching and laughing.

The dawn peeked a nosy head over the pine fringed hills as if it too was curious about her return to Loch Ness. She had missed this. The combination of sun and lake was more awe inspiring than Midas' touch and the magical key Mona needed to fulfill her contract.

"Desdemona Durant."

He said it like a Scottish cat who had found a fresh plate of haggis, the soft burr in his voice savoring each syllable of her name. Mona wasn't surprised he had learned of her arrival already. He may have played the part of the mere sexy pub owner, but she had learned the hard way that Lenox Sinclair was more than he appeared.

"Lenny," Mona said in mock cheerfulness as she deposited her Ghost Busters backpack on the pebbled mud shore next to her fishing rod and leaned against a boulder to slip a pair black galoshes over her Nikes. She gave his long, swimmer's body an assessing once over with an obvious hesitation at his crotch. "Looks like that rash finally cleared up. You're not hobbling at all anymore."

His long lipped mouth stretched into a smile, revealing crisp white teeth. "You always did have to be on top, didn't you?"

"No." She stood up and gave each galosh a final stomp to settle them into place. "You were just meant to be on bottom."

Lenox's eyes, no longer matching the morning mist curtaining the lake, sharpened to a cerulean blue-gray, a color only achieved from anger or arousal. She knew it wasn't arousal. That part of their relationship had been drawn, quartered and burned at the stake a year ago.

"I thought I had made it clear you were no longer welcome in Inverness," he said, his voice dropping to a dangerous low as he advanced towards her.

She took an instinctual step back into the peat-filled tide, the splash punctuating her weakness in the Baltic air. She covered the move by gathering her equipment. "I'm not in Inverness." She hooked a thumb at the crumbling Urquhart Castle a few hun-

dred feet over and up from where they stood. "I be-
lieve this location is closer to Drumnadrochit than Inverness."

"A technicality."

"A fact." She strode past him as if he wasn't there
and dropped the backpack, its weight indenting the
soft ground. "Besides, if I wanted to--"

"Why else would you be here?"

"I have a job," she said matter-of-factly as she released the fishing rod's hook to fly freely forward.

He gave her a look that said she was lying to one
of them.

"Your presence here already has some people
reaching for their pitchforks."

"I haven't set a foot in Inverness."

"Aye, but the loch is a fine line you're daring to
cross, and burning down half of someone's homet-
own has the tendency to make people . . . edgy."

It had been her home, too. She was American
blood but Scottish heart.

"It was only a third," she corrected, "and I didn't
set the town on fire."

Lenox arched a Celtic black eyebrow at her.

"Okay, it was my flamethrower, but it was the ban-
shee that torched the church."

"Ri-ight," he drawled.

At his sarcasm, her paper heart gained another
tear. She told herself she didn't care if he believed her
or not. She was here to do a job. That simple.

"So what task brings you to the loch?"  Lenox's voice was almost friendly-like as he crouched beside her and played with the backpack's cinched opening. Mona slapped his hand.  He laughed, deep and musically.  "Apprehending the fabled Loch Ness monster?"

"Not exactly."

"So you think you'll be the one to finally capture the beasty, Nessie, do ya, petal?"  He chuckled.  "With what?  A fishing pole and pixie dust?"

"No."  Mona opened the backpack and withdrew a rectangular can.  "A fishing pole and Spam."

"You Yanks and your canned meat."  Lenox laughed all out now.  "And you wonder why people doubt your sanity, Desdemona."

Mona ignored him and secured the processed pork product to the end of the line.  She swung the sagging pole behind her--half hoping to smack Lenox with it-- and cast her bait into the loch's murky waters.

With the exception of another rustle or two from behind them, they stood in silence, both waiting to see if she would sink or swim.  As the time ticked on, closing on the prime time to woo the unbelievable to show itself, Lenox had had enough.

"Petal, summon the sliver of sense you have left in that fanciful mind of yours and leave Scotland now."  He turned from her and sauntered inland.  "You'll never be welcome in Inverness again."

Tears heated Mona's eyes and fell to salt her lips. The fishing rod began to dip with her spirit when the water fifty feet out stirred and there was a tug on her line. And then another. Stronger. Smiling, Mona walked fully into the water to ease the line's tension before finally offering up bait, pole and all.

There was the rushing sound of a waterfall as the loch's waves parted for what ascended out of it. She barely heard Lenox's muttered, "What the bloody--," as she herself stood speechless at the sight.

At some point, her arm jerked as someone placed a wadded pound in her hand. She looked down and met the smiling prepubescent face of her client before he ran off shouting, "See, Craig, I told you so."

Her job was done.

The creature, finished with her luncheon treat, disappeared into the water, but Lenox remained a statue of shock. Mona laughed and tucked the pound in the waistband of his trousers. "Consider that the deposit on my tab. Inverness can make a girl real thirsty."

###

## About the Author

Amanda Buxton is a soon to be mother and marketing student with a love for paranormal and mystery/suspense fiction.

The author acknowledges the trademarks for Ghost Busters and Nike.

# Turning of the Tides
## by Jo-Anne Russell

The half-moon reflected in the dazzling blue-green of the ocean. Morrigan felt the sand pushing up between her toes as the tide washed over her feet. She wasn't supposed to be there, not at this time of night. She had heard the legends told by her parents and grandparents, legends of the Nixies and how they lured victims into the water to their death, but they were just myths.

Getting caught there didn't matter, nothing mattered except the decision she had to make. She placed her hand over the large swell of her womb. No one knew of course except for Adam – after all, he was the father; but he left her when he found out about the baby. The choice was hers alone, and the future of both her and her child would be determined tonight.

Morrigan watched the waves break the surface of the water. She closed her eyes and took in a deep breath of the salty air.

"Are you lost child?"

The woman's voice rang out like a sweet melody. Morrigan looked up. A beautiful woman in a white dress stood before her. Her feet were bare and the hem of her dress dripped with water.

"No, I know where I am."

The woman smiled and pulled her long golden hair from her face.

"I mean you look lost, or rather deep in thought. May I sit with you?"

Morrigan nodded, and stared back out over the ocean.

"My name is Aaleigh, what is yours?"

"Morrigan," she said, glancing briefly at her.

"Well my dear, you are quite young to be with child. Is that what brought you here?"

"Is it that easy to see?" Morrigan pulled her sweatshirt further down past her waist.

"No dear, you are hiding it well. I just have a gift for these matters. He will come early."

"He?"

"The child is male."

Morrigan felt the sting as her eyes welled with tears. It was so much easier to think of him as it, to separate herself from him, until she could figure out what to do. "Please tell me Aaleigh, will he have a good life?"

Aaleigh smiled. She took Morrigan's free hand in hers.

I can tell you he will grow to be a strong man one day, but only if you give him the life he deserves. You know that in your heart you are too young to raise him. You must give him to someone who will provide for him."

Morrigan pulled her hand free. A seething chill spread from her fingers to the length of her arm. She stood and rubbed it.

"If I keep him, I have to tell my parents. I have no choice."

"No," she said as she stood. "I mean, that would not be wise. Why burden your parents with something they would never forgive you for? I can help you find a worthy caregiver for him." Aaleigh placed her hands on Morrigan's shoulders.

Morrigan felt Aaleigh's grip tighten. She yanked herself free and took a few steps back. Panic swept through her, as she searched for an escape.

Aaleigh glared at her but instead of threatening words, a melody escaped her lips.

Morrigan felt her eyes tire and her body relax. She listened to the tune and soon Aaleigh's lullaby even drowned out the sound of the crashing waves. She watched the Nixie pass around her, walking backwards into the water. She followed, helpless to do more than will her feet to stop. The ocean waves crashed against her thighs, and in the distance, she thought she heard her mother's voice whispering her name.

Something strong had her by the neck from behind. It pulled her back toward the shore, but her body fought to move forward. Inside her mind was numb, focused only on Aaleigh and the force that pulled her deeper into the water.

Her father screamed in her ear as he moved his grip to her chest from under her arms. It lifted her and started dragging her backwards.

A blur passed in front of her and a new song began. She saw another woman before her as her vision cleared, singing a song she recognized from her childhood. Her head started to clear, and her father's voice yelled at her to get out of the water.

As the distance grew between her and the women, her body became her own again,

Aaleigh lashed out striking the other woman and dove under the water. The other woman turned and in a moment, a new panic spread through Morrigan as she saw her own mother's face before it too disappeared under the waves.

"Mother, no!" A crushing pain seized her womb as the words left her lips. She grabbing her belly as her legs gave way underneath. Her father's grip tightened and he pulled her the last few feet onto the land.

Waves crashed against her shaking knees, and a golden glow burst from the water.

"He is mine," Aaleigh screeched, reaching for her.

Behind Aaleigh, her mother surfaced. A rage covered her face like Morrigan had never seen before.

Another pain overtook Morrigan, as her mother grabbed Aaleigh by the hair, and thrust her free hand into Aaleigh's neck. A loud gurgle escaped along with a trail of thick black blood, as her mother ruthlessly tore out the Nixie's throat.

Pains ripped through Morrigan as her father carried her to a patch of grass. Her own screams echoed into the night as she gave birth with her mother and father by her side.

Her mother cradled the baby in her sweater as she looked sternly down at Morrigan.

"When he is old enough, you must warn him of the Nixie as we warned you," her mother said.

She looked at her son as he lay sleeping, in her mother's arms.

*"I will," she promised, "but will he listen?"*

### ###

## About the Author

Jo-Anne Russell is a horror writer living in Lindsay, Ontario Canada.

Her taste for the macabre has provided her imagination with a feast that fuels her writing and creativity. If you like horror, the bizarre, or you just don't like to sleep at night, give her books and short stories a try.

Her debut novel The Nightmare Project is the first in the shocking trilogy called Dangerous Minds, and is now available.

Find out more at http://www.jo-annerussell.ca

# One More Year
## by Jamie DeBree

"Tell me it's not true," Carrie said, brushing a tear from her cheek. The wind whipped violently through her hair as she watched his face, looking for any signs of dishonesty. "Tell me you're lying, damn it."

His gray eyes were calm – annoyingly so. He shrugged, looking out over the waves as they roared behind her. Of course he wouldn't look her in the eye. Traitor.

"I wouldn't lie about this." Rick's voice was soft. Smooth. The kind of voice that could seduce and soothe in the same breath. Many times she'd gotten lost in that sound, paying just enough attention to respond at the right places.

Not that she'd ever told him that. They were best friends after all. You didn't tell your best friend that his voice was an aphrodisiac.

Carrie turned her back, the angry roll of the water matching her mood. "Why didn't you tell me? Were you just going to leave without saying goodbye?"

Long arms slid around her, pulling her back
against that hard, sculpted chest. His scent surroun-
ded her, and she closed her eyes, breathing him in.

Maybe for the last time.

"I'd never do that," he murmured in her ear. "I
knew you'd be upset, and I didn't want to distract you
right before graduation." He rested his chin on her
shoulder, rocking her back and forth. "It's only for a
year, Carrie. We can email and do video chats. It will
be over before you know it, and I'll be back and
everything will be the same as it is now."

*That* was a lie. Even if he did come back, she knew
things would never be the same. He'd live his own
life, move on, maybe even find someone to love.
She'd move on too – she didn't want to, but that's
what people always did, wasn't it? From this moment
on, nothing would ever be the same between them,
and she hated that just as much as she hated her own
cowardice. Why couldn't she tell him she loved him,
that she wanted more?

She'd planned to once. Four years ago when they
were young and fresh out of high school. She'd lit
candles and made dinner in her tiny apartment because he'd said he had some exciting news to share
that night. When he knocked on the door she almost
couldn't breathe at the thought of finally telling him
how she really felt.

Then she'd seen the smiling pixie face behind him,
the linked fingers, and it was all she could do to set

another place at the table and listen to the story of how her best friend fell in love with someone else. It had nearly killed her. Six months later Rick's pixie was gone, but Carrie had accepted her role. She hadn't dared to dream of more since that night. She also hadn't bothered to date much in college, preferring his company when she could get it.

Now, standing here in Rick's arms the day before he left to explore another continent, her heart broke all over again. Clarity splashed over her like a glass of cold water, and she gently extricated herself from his embrace. He wasn't hers. He never had been, and she knew what she needed to do.

"You're right," she said, forcing a genuine smile as she turned to face him. "A year isn't that long, and we'll stay in touch." He smiled back at her, and she stared for a long moment, committing his face to memory. Then she rose up on her toes and lightly kissed his cheek.

"Goodbye, Rick," she said, taking a step back. "I hope you have a great trip." She turned to go, taking three steps before his voice arrested her flight.

"Meet me here," he said, pausing until she looked over her shoulder at him. "One year from today. I'll be waiting."

She hesitated. He didn't realize what he was asking. Not really. Finally she nodded. Then she walked away, not trusting herself to look back.

* * *

Three-hundred and sixty five days later, Carrie strolled out onto the old stone pier. Rick wouldn't be there, she knew, but it felt right to keep their last date. To honor the connection they'd shared.

She hadn't heard from him in several months, and the last time they'd spoken, he seemed uncomfortable. Strange, even. After that, her emails and calls had gone unanswered, though his parents assured her he was fine. She'd cried at first, heartbroken all over again. But as the weeks went by, she found a way to be happy. The hurt was still there, would probably always be. But today...today she'd say goodbye for good.

She stood at the water's edge, watching as the sun sank too fast over the gentle waves. In her hand, the first thing he'd ever given to her – a cassette tape of favorite songs long since copied to her hard drive. As the last vestiges of light slipped below the water, she flung the tape into the sea, and with it the hope she'd held close all these years.

*Five more minutes*, she thought wistfully. Shoving her hands into her pockets, she closed her eyes, the scent of salt and sand and...*him* engulfing her. When strong arms slipped around her from behind she smiled at the memory, reveled in the feel of her body against his just one more time. Even the breath on her neck felt the same.

"I love you, Carrie."

She opened her eyes, but the fantasy didn't disappear. Real arms held her close, real lips pressed soft kisses on the side of her neck. Somehow she pulled away, turning to see tired eyes shining under the dim wash of a distant streetlight.

"You came," she breathed. He pulled her close, his lips covering hers and despite the pain and heartbreak and questions, she clung to him. The past slipped away, and the only thing that mattered was here, now. Him.

One more year. This one would be different.

###

# About the Author

A full-time webmistress by day, Jamie DeBree writes steamy, action-packed romantic suspense late into the night. Her goal is to create the perfect blend of sensual attraction, emotional tension and fast-paced adventure, similar to the television crime dramas she's hopelessly addicted to.

Born in Billings Montana, she resides there with her husband and two over-sized lap dogs. She reads in a wide variety of genres including romance, erotica, action/adventure, thriller, horror and literary fiction.

For information on upcoming books, visit JamieDeBree.com.

# Never Forget
## by Heidi Sutherlin

"Never forget."

The words panted through her mind even as her lips remained closed.

"Never forget."

She'd forgotten.

She'd become comfortable, complacent. She was a woman bred for combat, whose only home had been a bunker run by a military branch that didn't exist. How many times had they reminded her and the other children that they were weapons not people? She didn't even have a name, at least not one that belonged only to her. And still she'd forgotten. She'd lowered her guard.

She stumbled on the wet rocks; the line of unseasonably high water of the lake ran orange along the shoreline. Cataloging the pain in her body, she ana lyzed the effects of her injuries and adjusted her pace accordingly. She knew she had at least another half an hour before her body would inevitably give in to the blood loss and trauma and begin to shut down.

She stumbled again and a ragged sound was pulled from her lips. It surprised her to realize it was a sob. Not slowing, she reached up to her face and felt the unfamiliar slickness of tears on her cheeks even as she pushed herself to continue her flight along the rocky beach.

Without pause she held one hand to her side, feeling the saturated cloth beneath her fingers. Then just as quickly she placed a finger to her neck, counting the erratic beats. Grimly, she processed the data. Even horribly injured she came to a stop with a fluid grace that some would mistake for a dancer's training, she scanned the area behind her. Her injuries would have toppled a normal agent. Instead, her body, altered first through genetics and then later with clever nanotechnology continued to move smoothly even as various systems began to slow and even shut down.

Lowering to a crouch that would make her nearly invisible to her pursuers, she mentally recalculated the distance to her possible exit. Rerunning strategies in her mind, she exhaled slowly with grim acceptance.

She would die here.

Accepting that outcome, she shifted the focus of her strategy from escape to collateral damage to the enemy. Feeling a slow and savage satisfaction at the thought, she welcomed the fire of battle that burned through the grief.

Scanning the area again, this time searching for a location that would allow her to go on the offensive, she spied two boulders about 500 feet ahead. There she would make her stand.

Reaching them, she closed her eyes and focused on bringing her body under the control that lifelong training and experimental genetics had given her. Instead, grief, love, and sorrow rose up to choke her. Fisting her hand in the twin gunshot wounds that gouged her side, she used the physical pain to force the grief to retreat. She was left gasping more from the breadth of her emotion than from the pain of what were certainly fatal wounds.

She knew it wasn't blood loss that had her feeling emotion she'd never before experienced. She felt love and grief in equal measure. Because of her, *he* was dead. She'd brought her enemies down upon the one person she'd ever dared to feel anything for. She didn't need to close her eyes as she forced herself to relive the moment the cabin had exploded.

She'd stepped outside to grab more wood for the fire. She'd only taken two steps back to the porch be fore a wall of fire had knocked her to the ground. She wouldn't remember screaming his name, only the unexpected pain of an ambush as she took two shots to the left side and another in her right thigh. They'd had the woods covered and so she'd been forced to retreat to the lake that lapped viciously at the shore in response to the storm even now building offshore. Her body, built for combat, hadn't slowed her, even as she'd left a trail of blood for her pursuers to follow.

The rustle of rocks sliding toward the water alerted her and her body poised for the attack. She identified the breathing of two men, one injured.

Injured?

She hadn't had a chance to return fire. She hadn't even had her weapon with her when she'd left the cabin.

There was another element involved.

One of her pursuers stepped around the boulder just as she shifted into a low crouch, hand to the ground. The leg she swept out was quick and vicious as it brought him down. Quickly and with little thought, her hands shot out to snap the bones of his neck before his body could fully settle to the ground. The swiftness of her attack cost her as the sickly wetness seemed to pour in a river down her side. She blinked away the black spots that danced in her vision.

Apparently, even a bionic woman had her limits, she thought with grim humor.

Sensing the second man, she attempted to stand only to stumble as he appeared around the smooth edge of the boulder. His gun raised and steady, he stood just out of reach and glanced over his fallen comrade. The weakness in her limbs made it clear that her body had finally betrayed her. She would never outrun a bullet.

There was no fear, only defiance as she raised her gaze to his emotionless one. Recognizing herself in his stance, she nodded once, not in defeat, but in professional acknowledgment.

Closing her eyes against the sudden nausea and dizziness, she heard the pop that signaled a silenced round. She was distantly surprised when she felt nothing. Not the pierce of the bullet, not the shock of its entry into her chest. Her mind had gone numb with the extent of her injuries and the expectation of death. She hit the ground as her legs lost their battle with gravity.

"Sweetheart? Open your eyes. Come on, open them for me."

Opening her eyes in astonishment, she looked up into his face. It was filled with savage triumph as she met his gaze. It turned instantly to a tenderness that caused her throat to tighten as he picked her up as gently as he could. His eyes were filled with love even as his mouth tightened into a grim line at her grunt of pain.

"How?" her voice was capable of nothing more than the single, loaded word.

"Backdoor, went to grab another blanket from the truck. Couldn't get to you in time. Backtracked for my equipment, by the time I made it I was too late to get more than a shot off before they clipped you and then I could only pin them down to give you a chance to get a head start." He was moving fast now, dodging trees expertly as he maneuvered through the forest to his vehicle.

"Who?"

"Me? CIA. Them? No clue."

"Why?" There was a new kind of pain now. Betrayal.

"At first? You were my assignment. Now? You're my reason to make it out of here. For getting up and surviving for another day." Somehow she knew the catch in his voice wasn't due to exertion and it warmed her even as the pain throbbed through her body with each step he took.

"I'm no one."

"Wrong. You're mine. Don't ever forget. You hear me? Mine."

"Never forget," she murmured as he shifted her slightly in his arms. She thought she heard him murmuring for back up and knew that she could relax. He'd take care of her.

*Mine*, he'd said.

*"Never forget."*

### 

## About the Author

Heidi Sutherlin is a writer of Romantic Suspense and Paranormal Romance, a Graphic Designer and a Cover Artist. She currently wreaks her particular brand of digital mayhem from her home in beautiful Central Oregon while riding herd on a wily four year old and a plastic addicted black lab named Frannie. To connect with Heidi, visit her web site at http://heidisutherlin.blogspot.co

# The Boatman
## by Jaimie Krycho

"Anna." Lara tried not to let the dread touch her voice.

"I should go with him."

"Anna, I thought we agreed that we would either stay or leave here together. You know I'm not joining the Boatman."

In the paling light, Anna glanced over her shoulder between strands of stringy auburn hair. Her face was empty, wraith like. Lara shivered. She willed herself, for the sake of their mutual promise, to try again. "Please, come inside. Reconsider."

The cold blowing in off the water seemed not to touch her friend at all. Anna turned her eyes back to the water, standing motionless on the sludgy beach as she had every night for many weeks now. Lara watched her fist open and close reflexively, crunching that wretched paper inside it.

If only the note had never come, Lara thought. If only the Boatman had never landed here. She re

membered the hubbub in her village the morning
Paul Stillman found the square of parchment nailed to
the rotting mooring post. He summoned family and
friends to the town square to read it, and those who
weren't present for the first reading soon saw the
note for themselves as it was passed from house to
house.

*If you want to be free,* it said, *come with me. Those who
have come before will welcome you. Every evening, I will wait.*

That was all – no signature, no farewell. But perhaps they had kept to themselves for too long,
huddled at the edge of the water, shunning the other
settlements inland, for Paul was quickly seduced by
the thought of leaving.

Lara had thought no one tried to stop him because
no decent person would admonish a grown man. Yet,
after the night the villagers saw Paul off into the
nameless boat, that black shell of a vessel on which
no one could spot the captain, many younger and
fresher than Paul chose to go as well.

Anna's betrothed was one of the last to depart,
after both Anna and Lara's families. Pleading had
done no good.

The thought prompted Lara to step closer to Anna
and place a slightly trembling hand on her shoulder.
"I know you miss Joseph, Anna. I don't think that go

ing with the Boatman will bring him back to you, though."

She started as Anna swatted her hand away. "Don't you understand? This is my only chance to find him and my family again! If you would give that up out of fear, you're worse than a coward!"

Lara smarted at the words, but all her tears were shed months past. She spoke only after a long while, with the wind wailing intermittently over the water. "At least let me stay with you until the boat comes."

She took Anna's silence as assent.

Long hours passed. The weak, cloud-covered sun chased shadows across the water until, with a blaze of gold, it gave up and lay down behind the horizon. The darkness stole over Lara and Anna's abandoned village, and Lara's fear grew with it. The tears began to reform in a deep cavern in her chest.

Finally, the night settled into its place. The darkness was profound. Day-wary creatures had just begun their quiet dirge when Lara spotted the boat.

The vessel seemed to come from nowhere, riding the mists that played on the water's foggy glass surface. It was as Lara remembered it – broken-looking planks like old teeth, and a moss-covered hull like a molding bread crust. It terrified her.

"Anna," she breathed, but Anna seemed not to notice.

Steadily, the boat cut its way to the shore. Lara took steps backward even as Anna remained fixed in place.

Soon the craft was close enough for Anna to touch. It turned parallel to the shore and stopped without a hand or rope appearing to moor it. Lara didn't see where the gangplank came from, but suddenly it was there.

Anna took a step forward, and desperation pushed the words tumbling out of Lara's mouth.

"Anna, *don't go!*"

Anna offered that same, wraith like glance over her shoulder for a final time in response, and Lara saw that her last friend had already gone.

Lara never saw the Boatman, of course. As soon as Anna boarded the vessel, she disappeared, too – melting into some fold of bleak magic that covered the world tonight. Lara stood on the shore, staring hollowly into the mists, feeling so utterly alone that all sorrow congealed into numbness.

There was nothing left here, nothing.

A wad of paper blew past Lara's feet, then, and she bent to pick it up. Unfolding it slowly, she knew the words even before she began to read them.

*If you want to be free, come with me. Those who have come before will welcome you.*

Lara felt a stab of pain, and bent over, holding her stomach, wishing the numbness had not stoppered her tears. Maybe Anna was right. How could she deny her one chance to be with those she loved?

She looked up at the sky, dark and darkened still by black scudding clouds. *Every evening, I will wait,* the Boatman had written. Though the pain did not subside, Lara tried to straighten as a new thought formed – now that she was alone, nothing stopped her from doing what she had urged her people not to.

Her feet seemed to carry her independent of her will to the spot where Anna had stood staring in evenings past. Until this moment, she had not believed there was a force stronger than fear.

The Boatman's freedom, whatever it was, was better than the void that was left for her here. She took off her shoes and dug her toes into sludgy beach. The cold blowing in off the water did not touch her at all.

###

## About the Author

Jaimie Krycho recently earned her BA in journalism/professional writing from the University of Oklahoma, and now resides in Norman, Oklahoma, with her husband. She has written several published short stories, including the Kindle anthology *Dangerous Dreamworlds* under pen name Morgan Locke. Jaimie is currently editing the final draft of her first fantasy novel. You can track her progress at jaimiekrycho.com.

## Rattles Flash Fiction

*In a Dark Place* (Oct. 2011)

*At the Water's Edge* (Nov. 2011)

*The Old Sofa* (Dec. 2011)

www.ingramcontent.com/pod-product-compliance
Lightning Source LLC
Chambersburg PA
CBHW020651130626
46552CB00003B/1502